Dear Parents:

Congratulations! Your child is taking the first steps on an exciting journey. The destination? Independent reading!

STEP INTO READING® will help your child get there. The program offers five steps to reading success. Each step includes fun stories and colorful art or photographs. In addition to original fiction and books with favorite characters, there are Step into Reading Non-Fiction Readers, Phonics Readers and Boxed Sets, Sticker Readers, and Comic Readers—a complete literacy program with something to interest every child.

Learning to Read, Step by Step!

Ready to Read Preschool–Kindergarten
• big type and easy words • rhyme and rhythm • picture clues
For children who know the alphabet and are eager to begin reading.

Reading with Help Preschool–Grade 1
• basic vocabulary • short sentences • simple stories
For children who recognize familiar words and sound out new words with help.

Reading on Your Own Grades 1–3
• engaging characters • easy-to-follow plots • popular topics
For children who are ready to read on their own.

Reading Paragraphs Grades 2–3
• challenging vocabulary • short paragraphs • exciting stories
For newly independent readers who read simple sentences with confidence.

Ready for Chapters Grades 2–4
• chapters • longer paragraphs • full-color art
For children who want to take the plunge into chapter books but still like colorful pictures.

STEP INTO READING® is designed to give every child a successful reading experience. The grade levels are only guides; children will progress through the steps at their own speed, developing confidence in their reading. The F&P Text Level on the back cover serves as another tool to help you choose the right book for your child.

Remember, a lifetime love of reading starts with a single step!

For the amazing Heidi Kilgras and Tim Bowers
—J.H.

Text copyright © 2017 by Joan Holub
Cover art and interior illustrations copyright © 2017 by Tim Bowers

Visit us on the Web!
StepIntoReading.com
randomhousekids.com

Educators and librarians, for a variety of teaching tools, visit us at RHTeachersLibrarians.com

Library of Congress Cataloging-in-Publication Data
Names: Holub, Joan, author. | Bowers, Tim, illustrator.
Title: Vampoodle / Joan Holub, Tim Bowers.
Description: New York : Random House, [2017] | Series: Step into reading. Step 2 |
Summary: Dogs, including Vampoodle—a poodle with fangs—enjoy Halloween fun.
Identifiers: LCCN 2015043656 (print) | LCCN 2016019633 (ebook) |
ISBN 978-1-101-93666-5 (trade pbk.) | ISBN 978-1-101-93667-2 (lib. bdg.) |
ISBN 978-1-101-93668-9 (ebook)
Subjects: | CYAC: Stories in rhyme. | Dogs—Fiction. | Poodles—Fiction. |
Vampires—Fiction. | Halloween—Fiction.
Classification: LCC PZ8.3.H74 Vam 2017 (print) | LCC PZ8.3.H74 (ebook) | DDC [E]—dc23

Printed in the United States of America
10 9 8 7 6 5 4 3 2 1

This book has been officially leveled by using the F&P Text Level Gradient™ Leveling System.

Vampoodle

by Joan Holub
illustrated by Tim Bowers

Random House 🏠 New York

It's Halloween!
Ears prick up.
"Who is here?"
barks poodle pup.

Doggies enter,
greeting friends.

6

Wag, wag, kiss.

Vampoodle grins.

To the backyard.

Stay awhile!

Time to party

puppy style!

Fetching, catching.

Pumpkin ride.

Tug-of-war

on grass outside.

Bob for weenies.

Slobber, chew.

Come back, pug.

We want some, too!

Frisky romping.

Yappy chat.

Sudden stop.

Woof! Who is that?

Monster comes
with mummy white.
Bumblebee,
robot, and knight.

Zombie holding
out a sack.
Will Vampoodle
be his snack?

Dogs retreat at
super speed.
Scaredy-poodle
takes the lead.

Shaking, quaking.

Back inside.

Zipping, tripping.

Run and hide!

Laundry spilling
everywhere!
Socks and towels
fly through the air!

Underwear hat,
tutu, cape.
Yum—a slipper!
Pups escape!

Sillies,

do not be afraid.

Come out for the dog parade!

Blinking leashes.

Tags that shine.

Pups get costumes.

Looking fine.

Hairy fairy.

Pug bullfrog.

Flower power.

Underdog.

Ballerina.

Superfly.

Princess pooch.

Vampoodle guy!

Dogs show off.
Then, one by one,
they head home.
Their day was fun.

Cutest critters

ever seen.

Happy Doggy
Halloween!